HUSH UP
and hibernate!

Designed by Patricia Mitter

ISBN 978-1-943978-36-6

Printed in Canada

10 9 8 7 6 5 4 3 2 1

Published by Persnickety Press
120A North Salem St
Apex, NC 27502
www.Persnickety-Press.com

cpsia tracking label information
Production Location: Friesens Corporation,
Altona, Manitoba, Canada
Production Date: 6/15/2018
Cohort: Batch № 244542

*"For Amiee Snyder and all the children
of Williams Elementary School,
Jonesville, Michigan."*

–S.M.

HUSH UP
and hibernate!

by Sandra Markle

Illustrated by Howard McWilliam

PERSNICKETY PRESS

Mama Bear lifts her head and looks at
red leaves dancing in the wind.

"I see winter coming,"
she tells her cub.
"It's time to hibernate."

"But, Mama,"
Baby Bear says.
"I'm hungry."

HONK!

HONK!

Mama Bear grunts. "I guess we can eat a little longer before we sleep away the winter." Side-by-side, they munch chokecherries until a flock of geese flies past.

Mama Bear slowly lifts her big head and listens to their honking.

"I hear winter coming," she tells her cub.
"It's time to hibernate."

"But, Mama," Baby Bear says.
"I'm thirsty."

So Mama Bear leads her cub through
the woods and down to the lake.

When a fish swims past, Baby Bear tries to catch it but

MISSES!

"I think that fish is in a hurry to hibernate," he says.
Mama Bear snorts. "Fish don't hibernate.
Neither do the voles, the owls, or the rabbits."

"No fair! Baby Bear says.
"Why can't I stay up all winter?"

Mama Bear sighs. "Because, when winter comes, there won't be any chokecherries for you to eat. No grubs or bugs. No fish either because the lake freezes over."

Baby Bear stamps his feet.
"I don't care. I'll find food somewhere."

Mama Bear says, "There's another
reason winter's not for baby bears."

STOMP!

STOMP!

"Hungry wolves don't hibernate. They hunt all winter long.

GROWL!

GROWL!

So do mountain lions. They might catch you without me to keep you safe."

"You won't be with me?" Baby Bear's jaw drops.

"Where will you be?"
"I'll be hibernating," Mama Bear says as she plods off.

Baby Bear stays—but only for a minute—
because looking around he sees the woods is full of shadows.
Could wolves be hiding there?
Or mountain lions?

Baby Bear runs as fast as he can to catch up with Mama.
When they reach their den under the big, old tree, they crawl in and curl up.

But Baby Bear
wiggles.

Mama Bear puffs,
"What's wrong now?"

"I can't hibernate,"
Baby Bear says.
"This bed is too hard."

So the bears crawl out of their den.
Mama Bear paws more leaves inside
until snowflakes fill the air.

"Winter's here," she tells her cub.
"It really IS time to hibernate."

"But, Mama," Baby Bear says.
"I can't hibernate yet."

"I have to say goodbye to the fish. The moose. The owls. The rabbits. And the voles. I'll go fast and hurry back."

Baby Bear trots off.

Mama Bear charges to catch up. Roars,

"ENOUGH!"

Then she nudges her cub back into their den. And nose-to-nose with him says, "Now, hush up and hibernate till spring!"

With the winter wind howling outside,
Mama Bear and Baby Bear curl up, side-by-side.

And *hibernate.*

SNORE! SNORE!

SNORT! SNORT!

GRUNT!

"Mama Bear?" Baby Bear
whispers in her ear.
"Can you hear me?"

Mama Bear snuffles.
"What is it, dear?"

"Is it spring yet?"

DO BEARS REALLY HIBERNATE?

Hibernating is the way some animals survive times when food is hard to find. People usually say bears hibernate. Scientists explain bears have a special kind of hibernation they call a winter sleep. The main difference is that a bear's body temperature only drops a little below normal. The body temperature of other hibernators drops a lot—usually to just above freezing. This difference is why a bear can wake up quickly and react to danger. Other hibernators have to warm up, which happens fairly slowly, before they can become active.

However, there are other important differences between a bear's winter sleep hibernation and just sleeping. So, what if you could hibernate the way a bear does? Could you do it? Take this quiz to find out!

COULD YOU HIBERNATE LIKE A BEAR?

Could you go without eating anything for about 100 days?

A BEAR DOES!

Could you go without drinking anything for about 100 days?

A BEAR DOES!

Could you skip peeing or pooing for about 100 days?

A BEAR DOES!

Could you breathe just once a minute?

A BEAR DOES! That's down from a bear's normal 6 to 10 breaths per minute. To compare, count about how many breaths you take sitting still for one minute.

WHERE ARE THE OTHER HIBERNATORS?

Where might you find other animals hibernating in the story's forest setting? Read about these other animals. Then look back through the story. Where might you find them safe and sound, hibernating through the winter?

Photo by sirtravelalot/Shutterstock

YELLOW-BELLIED MARMOT In the spring and summer, it eats plants: leaves, flowers and seeds. And it digs shallow burrows to stay safe while it rests. To get ready for winter, it burrows much deeper underground—15 feet or more—to be below where the ground freezes. It usually hibernates from about September to May.

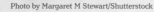
Photo by Margaret M Stewart/Shutterstock

CHIPMUNK It digs a deep, wintertime burrow system under rocks or logs. This has tunnels and chambers. One chamber has dry leaves for the chipmunk's bed. And there are food chambers stocked with grasses and seeds it carried there in its cheeks. Plus, there are other chambers to deposit wastes. From time-to-time during the winter, the chipmunk becomes active, eats, and passes wastes. It usually hibernates from October to mid-March.

Photo by Steve Bower/Shutterstock

SNAPPING TURTLE While hibernating, it is able to survive without breathing for as long as 5 months. So, it usually burrows into the muddy bottom of a pond or lake. And it stays there, underwater, where it's a little warmer than freezing cold. It usually hibernates from late October to March.

Photo by SDeming/Shutterstock

GARTER SNAKE In spring and summer, it stays near water and eats mainly frogs, slugs, and earthworms. As the weather cools, it stops eating and crawls into a den space under rocks or tree stumps. It often hibernates with lots of other garter snakes. It usually hibernates from October through March.

DEN LIKE A BEAR

Just follow these steps to pretend you're a bear getting ready to den for the winter.

 1 You'll need a large box with the opening flaps removed. Or cover a small table with blankets so there are walls on all sides. Then fold up one corner to make a small opening. This should create a space just right for you to curl up inside. A bear chooses a den that's just a little bit larger than its body. That way there won't be a lot of cold air blowing around it. It may even choose a den where snow is likely to blanket the opening.

 2 While not all bears make a bed, follow Mama Bear's example and add a bed to your den. Use crumpled up clean packing paper or wrapping paper in place of leaves. Pile the paper outside the den door and push it inside, the way a bear would.

 3 Crawl into your den. Curl up with your back to the door. That's what a bear does. It's a way to let your body help block out cold winds. And help you stay warm.

Okay get comfy. Because, if you den like a bear, you'll be snug inside your den for the next 100 days!

EXPLORE MORE Check out these books and websites to discover even more.

Alinsky, Shelby. *National Geographic Readers: Sleep, Bear!* (Washington, D.C.: National Geographic, 2015). Follow a bear cub getting ready to hibernate.

Kosara, Tori. *Scholastic Reader Level 2: Hibernation.* (New York, Scholastic, 2012). Investigate different kinds of hibernating animals.

Markle, Sandra. *Growing Up Wild: Bears.* (New York: Atheneum, 2000). Compare the lives of different kinds of bears as they grow up and live through every season in their habitat.

National Geographic Kids: Brown Bear
kids.nationalgeographic.com/animals/brown-bear/#brown-bear-cubs.jpg
Discover something special that can happen while a female bear is asleep for the winter.

Watch, Know, Learn
watchknowlearn.org/Video.aspx?VideoID=27543&CategoryID=7557
Watch a short video of a bear hibernating. It doesn't just sleep!

Nova: Bear Essentials of Hibernation
pbs.org/wgbh/nova/nature/bear-essentials-of-hibernation.html
Take a close look at black bears: how they get ready to hibernate; where they hibernate; how their bodies change during hibernation.

Bear hibernation facts reviewed by Kerry Gunther, Bear Management Biologist. Yellowstone National Park.